MW01643884

Anywhere but the Bed: A Series of Short Stories and Poems

by Alise Merwin-Rasberry

Published by Made 4 This (318) 406-2249
Edited by Jhordynn of Made 4 This
Cover designed by Black Market CEO
Cover formatted by Psalmyy of Fiverr

ISBN (paperback): 978-1-7365773-2-5

Table of Contents

Table of Contents

Dedicated to my first love: One interaction with you always can inspire me to write. I never thought I'd meet my muse at a house party in the 11th grade.

I always get more than I can handle.

My Mouth

My whole mouth wants to please you.

Wake you up with kisses,

Say encouraging words to you on a bad day,

Speak kindness and inspiration to your ideas

Keep it closed about the secrets between us

Pick out shades of lipstick that look good wrapped around your dick

Choke on it until it's all the way down my throat

Whisper arousing words to get you in the mood

Lick the mess up we create

No Sleep

We are always talking shit through text messages. We didn't let the distance put our fires out, or so I thought.

I'd send a picture of the breakfast I cooked with the caption, "If you were here, this would be your breakfast."

He would reply, "If you were here, you'd be my breakfast."

Work was stressful that day. So, I texted,
Can I have a hug?

He texted back, ***sure***.

The distance never stopped the fantasy.

Then he texted, ***WYD after work?***

I have so much to do after. My day has been so long.

I thought nothing of it.

I hoped you would be doing me. Then he sent a screenshot his flight arrival time.

The airport seemed full of people when I went to pick him up. We didn't care. He kissed me just like Whitney and Kevin in The Bodyguard, and I couldn't wait to kiss him like Karrine in the bed. He got in the car, and I rubbed his dick through those damn gray sweat pants. Yes, he wore them.

We got a hotel room.

I couldn’t keep my lips off him. We had barely closed the door before I was in a three-point stance being a homecoming present.

We both washed up. He wanted to take a tour of the city. He hadn't been home in a while. I got dressed and obliged him, but I was really trying to get my back blown out.

We went out to eat. The conversation was like he never moved away. We got to the club. I grinded on him on the dance floor trying to let him know what he could have. I wanted to go back to the room to have him to myself, by myself; this was just another pit stop.

We needed more supplies. The closest supply store to us was the store connected to the strip club. Thc store gave us free passes to get in the strip club when we checked out, so we ended up in the strip club.

He pointed out a woman, looked at me, and said, "Would you?"

"Of course."

He was always testing to see if I wasn't bullshitting about a threesome. He got a lap dance from the mystery lady he pointed out. It turned me on, and now I was ready to go! My clit throbbed. I could almost taste my dessert.

He <u>Bronx Tale</u> door tested me, but when I opened the car door, I told him to pull his dick out. I sucked him through the door right in the parking lot. I wanted it bad. The emergency brake was poking my rib cage, and I locked the steering wheel when I reached for it to scoot up.

"Get in," I told him.

It was getting late. I had it made up in my mind that I could work remote tomorrow. I slipped on lingerie in the bathroom. I don't know why I would prolong this man giving me orgasms. When I stepped into the room, he was already naked and erect on the bed.

"Damn, you so fine. I missed you," he whispered into my soul.

I straddled and kissed him. He looked at me like he was lucky to have me. He seemed enamored with my beauty my body.

"Sit on my face."

He undid my teddy with his teeth. I was impressed. He ate my treasure like he had something to prove, giving me my first orgasm of the night. See, he was the one who introduced me to multiples. I used to be one and done, but not anymore ever since him. So, now in the back of my mind, I was trying to keep an accurate cum count. It seemed like he was always trying to add one, or it was just getting easier. I was so aroused, and I wanted to touch my prize with that big G-spot finder he called a dick. He never seemed to mind that I couldn't go as long as him when we did 69.

That was two.

I got off him. I kissed me off his lips. He laid me down and stared for second.

"All this mine?" he asked me.

He had some game. He penetrated me gently. He knew how tight I was, so he always took his time. But as soon as I opened up, that was the green light. My legs went over his shoulders, and he pounded me. After his third pounding, I came.

That's three.

Pound, pound, pound.

Four.

Pound, pound, pound.

Five.

There was a puddle forming on the sheet. It was so intense that those three words slipped off my lips. I wanted to take them back. But euphoria had him in another dimension; I don't think he heard me. If he did, he didn't let on about it.

I scratched his back to help myself endure the intense pleasure, but it didn't work. I tried to slide from underneath. I put my hand around his bald head and took a few more strokes. I needed a second to revamp. I tapped and scratched his back to get his attention. He took the cue and stopped. I laid on my side, and we spooned, but the break was short-lived. We both wanted more. He lifted my thighs up, slipped inside, and we were back at it.

Six.

I was about to stop counting. He straddled my thigh and put the other over his shoulder. *Shit. What kind of wrestling move...?*

He got up.

"Come here," he growled.

I stood and leaned over the bed with my legs spread. I gripped the sheets. He was so deep. I screamed. I reached for a pillow to scream.

"Don't cover your mouth! Fuck it, I want you to be heard!"

He reached for the pillow and tossed it across the room. I gave him strokes mainly to slow him down. It turned him on more. How did I get such a freak?

Seven came when I used my hand to pull his dick out for a second.

Eight came when he stuck it back in. *I'm here for it.*

Nine came, and my legs quivered.

I fell, and he landed laying on top of my back. We laughed, saying, "Damn." He flipped my legs back onto the bed, and I really, really thought I was done.

"I don't think I can cum no more."

"I think you can. Get on all fours."

He slid me to the edge of the bed and started eating my pussy from the back while he was sitting on the floor. It felt like his whole face was in it. His nose pushed my lips open, and his tongue tickled my senses.

Ten. Or so I thought. I lost count.

Ten's a good number.

I crawled off his face. I sat on the edge of the bed and sucked his dick. I hate to admit it, but his dick was so big my jaws hurt. But I kept going, trying not to choke. I guided it further and further down my throat until it triggered my gag reflex. *Relax and breathe.*

I liked going up to the tip of his dick and flicking my tongue because I could taste a little of the cum coming out. That might be nasty, but this was not the time to worry about that. He didn't want to cum from me sucking his dick. I could tell because it felt like I had been sucking his dick forever, and he was still hard. It grew in in my mouth. I liked that feeling, too.

Ah, here it comes.

“That pussy too good. Lay back down.”

He started rubbing my clit like it was a joystick or an Xbox controller. I felt my nipples become erect. My back stretched. Fuck counting. At this point, I flipped and crawled towards the headboard. He was so focused. We saw dawn peaking through the curtains.

“Can I get mine?” he asked me.

He laid me flat and went inside of me. He came on my back. He shook his penis and went back in. I was surprised.

Orgasm number unknown.

He said, “You should try to rest. You have work, and this starts my vacation.”

He cleaned his love juice off me. I placed my booty on him while laying naked in bed; I was half asleep. He stroked me slowly, grabbing my tummy. I dozed off.

A few hours later, the concierge called, saying we overstayed the checkout time, and the hotel was booked solid for the next night. We had to go.

But to where?

The Dream

Last night, I dreamed I lost you. You weren't dead, but it was like I couldn't reach you. I woke up crying.

I didn't want to tell you 'cause it
seemed sad, but I have to say this.

I just wanted to tell the reasons you will always be in my heart. You changed my life for the better. Helped me realized who I am as a woman. You didn't shame me for my secrets, which made it easier for me to deal with my shit.

I have been happy with us and no outside influences fucking up what we got going on.

You are the best lover I have ever had. You take me to ecstasy. Even if we give our hearts to other people down the road, you will always have this spot with me.
I love you.

-Your princess

Touch

I've run my fingers over diamonds and held
priceless antiques

Worn cashmere and silk and felt the
warmness of heated leather seats

I've held teddy bears while being surrounded
by pillows and blankets

I’ve caressed chilled glasses of wine at the
end of a stressful day

But nothing compares to laying in your arms
and hearing your heartbeat in my ear.

But you, My Dear, are by far my favorite
thing to touch.

I feel you like the intensity of a magnet to metal
Magical mood altering sensory overload

I feel you when you are not here

I feel you even when you are not here

The Couch

You ever get to the point in your sex life where you say, “Anywhere but the bed”?

He’s home! Cue the Jill Scott…we going to have to connect some music.

We’d been kicked out of the hotel, but while he was home, I wanted to make him nutt as many times as possible. Every time he nutted, it made me purr like the sexy cat I imagined myself to be.

I picked this particular couch to go in my new house. It had a cute vintage feel, but it was sturdy. Or so I thought.

The slight pop of the wood going in and out of place should have had me more cautious, but it was feeding our ecstasy. I felt his intensity pick up with every clap of the wood. We were sucked into the rhythm.

I was on my third orgasm when I went full Chappelle Show and said, “but this was my couch!” I was kneeling on the couch, halfway over the armrest, and a knee anchored on the floor. It was so intense. He bunched my skirt up and used it as a grip. He got closer, used my bra strap as an anchor, and I spread my knees wider. His dick went further and deeper inside. I yelled out in extreme passion.

My bra strap was stretchy, not making for a good stable anchor. I could tell he wanted to grab my hair, but he knew it was a wig, and he gave me the respect of not pulling it; he gripped the back of my neck instead. He reached and squeezed my neck just a little.

I came.

I heard him moan, “Man, that shit good.”

I could feel him quiver. It boosted my confidence, so I clenched his dick inside me and let it go. *Cum for me, Baby.*

Goodbye: I miss you Text/10 Questions

I don't want to listen to any music!

I don't want a soundtrack to feeling like this.

10 years as friends.

4 years as lovers.

We're supposed to miss each other.

But we can't ignore the fact that you moved on.

You chose to be with someone else.

No matter how we feel with each other,

You have to be willing to dial it back for your own happiness.

So when you text you miss me... I know.

Don't say you miss me for my sake.

I don't need it.

I don't want to be drawn back into something you ended.

I'm trying to deal with it on my own like a mature human being.

You turned me into something I never wanted to be— a jealous woman.

It gives me no joy to know that I can distract another woman's man.

How can you be my every thought and I
barely cross your mind?

Did you mean any of it?

Am I crazy?

Did I read between the lines?

Do you remember what you said?

Does "I love you" mean something
different to you?

Did I miss the warning signs?

Do you remember you said it first?

How could you hurt me?

Why is it so easy for you to move on?

The DJ

It was my third career and third degree and I thought I'd never get a job in my home town, but I was excited to have landed a paid internship at the first radio station in the city. There was a lot to absorb. I grew up listening to this station; I love radio.

My program manager let me know that our biggest sponsor was a Mexican restaurant. It was the unspoken rule that you should go to Taco Tuesdays to network and meet industry people. Though I was anxious, I made sure I was Happy Hour cute. I wore my soft leather skirt that was just short and tight enough to be almost inappropriate for work. The blouse was sheer, and the bow rested right on my cleavage.

I got there super early. I was planning to only shake a few hands and leave. I was given my first big deadline: have my show recorded by 11 p.m. If I went to happy hour from 4:30 to 6:30, I could make it back to the station with plenty of time learn the soundboard to record the show.

I was the first one at Taco Tuesdays, and the bar was a little quiet. The tequila was only $2, so I decided I'd loosen myself up a bit. I was focused on the sports on the TV when I heard the bartender yell, "Miiiike!" with enthusiasm. I glanced out the corner of my eye and then back at TV. I felt the body of someone sitting on the bar stool next to me.

"Yo, give me two of them," the man over my shoulder said.

His voice ran down my spine, and I immediately recognized who he was. DJ D-Mic. His voice was sexy, and in person, he was even sexier.

Here I go. Butterflies.

"Hi. I'm new to the radio group. I recognized your voice."

"Well, I'm Michael. How they treating you?"

"I have my first show due tonight, so I'll be leaving. I just wanted to show my face."

He laughed at my not answering his question. He was so nice to look at. I hiked my skirt up even further and crossed my legs to show them off.

He bought me a shot. I was traveling further down Tequila Path than I would like. He seemed to know everyone who walked by. We laughed and talked with the crowds of people coming in and out the taco bar. The tequila made me the perfect social butterfly.

It was 7:45 p.m. when he said, “I’m getting out of here. My ride share is on the way.”

“Oh shit,” I said in a panic. “I had too much fun, and I have to do the show.”

“I'll help you with the show since I got you tore up your first Taco Tuesday.”

I jumped up to follow him to the Lyft. He walked so quickly. I reached out and grabbed him because the drinks had me wobbly. The embrace was a little awkward, but I got a good feel of what I had been looking at and fantasizing about all night.

When we got to the station, we went to his office.

He said, “Let me print you a prep sheet and a timing sheet from the shared drive right quick.”

The tequila was telling me that this was my chance to get what I really wanted. I leaned over his desk to look at his screen.

"How do I access that for myself?" I asked.

I was putting one hand on the desk and the other on his lap. I rubbed his dick through his slacks. He stared with a little shock and hesitance like he was still debating whether he was going to let it happen. I sat on the desk, unbuckled his pants, and stuck my hand inside.

"Close the door!" he belted.

I got up and did just that.

When I came back, I got down on my knees. I pulled it out of his pants.

"You know what you doing?" he asked me.

"Yea. I'm doing exactly what I want to be doing."

I let my mouth go all the way down until it hit the back of my throat on the first stroke, letting more and more of my saliva wet his penis as I came back to the tip and flicked my tongue ring back and forth. I felt him getting bigger in my mouth as I went up and down. I turned my head to the side and let it hit the back of my throat at an angle. He grew even more. He grew so much that I just knew I was going to choke. And I did.

After I recovered from choking, I got some good suction going, using my hand to match the stroke.

"Oh shit." He moaned my name.

Occasionally, things fell off the desk, letting me know he was about to cum.

I started thinking about the show.

“What time is it?” I asked.

“Don't worry about it.”

“The show!”

“Just keep going. I got you. I'm almost there.”

I kept going, but he wouldn’t cum.

“Michael!”

“Alright, alright. But damn, Girl.”

As we walked down the halls, I skimmed the paper he printed. I felt him smack me on the ass. I was wet, but I had to finish.

He opened the programs and worked the sound boards with ease. As he showed me how to record my segments in between the commercial break, I sat on his lap and felt his breath down my neck and ear. We were almost done recording— grabbing each other in between each moment of serious work.

During the last break, my skirt was hiked all the way up. I asked him to let me run through it by myself. He did. I stood up over the soundboard, and I attempted my last segment.

I felt him move my panties over. Following was the latex on his big penis going inside me. I gripped the soundboard, giving him his strokes back. I felt the rhythm from the ribbon on my blouse touching my bouncing breast.

I climaxed while working my segment, laying across the soundboard.

Checklist

Passion?

An understatement.

Your skin?

Alluring.

Phones?

Overheated, hooked to chargers.

Marathon calls.

Late check-outs.

Kisses as alarm clocks.

Secret looks.

Snickers from friends.

Broken hearts.

But no regrets.

The DJ: Part Two

The secret was fun to keep. It excited me to go to work at the station. As the intern, I did the traffic and weather at the top and bottom of the drive home hours. I was getting really familiar with the soundboard buttons. I laughed and reminisced sometimes about how the buttons I pressed had once pressed into my skin when D-Mic had me bent over them.

I was giddy passing him in the hall. If I got to work early enough, we had time to get it in, in the supply closet where we kept the station's promotional items. My favorite thing was to be on my knees under his desk giving him head.

"Have you seen the intern?" DJs would ask as they walked by his office.

It made me laugh; it made him nervous.

Perhaps it was too good. Maybe it was time to slow it down.

The Vow

I promise to be careful with the love you give.

For it is one earned inch-by-inch.

I will be deliberate and kind in my language— not taking for granted any words between us,

Protective of our bond hedged from the outside and fortified with good intentions,

Attentive to your needs and vigilant enough to know when I can meet them,

Watchful over the trust you give because it was hard built.

My vow is to love you with the least amount of conditions my human soul can give.

Three

We sit on the bed; we know why we are here. In my own way, I try to make a joke. Then I know for sure. I'm going to need some weed or Hennessy. Both. I'm not shy with the drinks or the blunt. I share anecdotes about the last time me and my friend Ursula got high. As I let out a cough in front of my lover Marcus, I tell her how crazy I was when I smoked a whole blunt by myself.

The weed's kicking in, and so are the butterflies in my stomach. I crawl towards Ursula and grab her by the hand. I know our friendship is about to change.

"Can I kiss you? You don't have to do anything you don't want to," I say to Ursula, calmly.

I turn to Marcus and ask, “Do you mind watching for now?”

I kiss her gently, no tongue, but then she goes for it.

I pause and turn and say, “I’m going to kiss him, too.” And I did.

I lay her down, kissing her as I reach in her sweat pants and feel for her clit. I’ve never been with a woman, but I figure I’ll do to her what I want done to me. I pull her sweats off, kiss her belly, then her lips again.

“Can we both with eat you?” I ask her.

Her sensual hisses are her *yes*.

I'm not excited about eating pussy. I have never done it, but it feels good to have an expert with me.

Here we go, I think to myself.

I lick her once, then take my fingers and peel back her lips to really get to her clit. I give it a good honest try, licking and sucking. I take three fingers and go inside. She's wet, and I feel it's my duty to make sure she is pleasured.

How did we get here? I think to myself. *I've convinced my best friend to join in my and my lover's adventure.*

I look up and over at Marcus who is lying on his back in the bed. He has his dick out. It's so big. I feel it's shaped just perfect to find my G-spot. I signal for him to come over. He rolls over slowly.

“I’m here, Ursula,” I say to her, like I’m a life coach, assuring her I’m not leaving her alone.

It's awkward, so he gets out the bed and pulls her to the edge. We both kneel on the floor and take turns eating her. I reach out to jack him off; I’m getting my fingers inside of Ursula when possible.

She says, “Oh, shit!”

She's cumming. Success.

I climb on the bed and get behind her. I sit her up and kiss her neck. She’s having fun. I reach around and rub her labia for reassurance.

“Let me lay back, and you get on top,” she tells me.

I'm wearing a lingerie top and see-through bottoms. I reach my leg over her face and neck. The sensation of her mouth is pleasing. I let it happen.

Marcus looks at me and says, "Bring that ass over here."

I crawl down Ursula's body and kiss him. I feel how wet I am when my lips come together from the crawl. *That's my lover coming for me*, I think to myself as Marcus meets me halfway. I'm reverse cow girl on Ursula, so I rub and grind on her and kiss him. We have always kissed passionately.

We both taste like weed and Ursula. I lick her off his lips and smile and look him in the eyes. I put my arms around his neck.

"You ready, Baby?" he asks. I nod *yes*. "Then turn over."

I'm now on all 4s on top of Ursula, facing her, and he rubs my pussy. He bounces his dick on my ass.

"That thang wet," he says.

He bends back down and eats my pussy from the back. I cum hard, and with all my might I try not to collapse on her. He rubs my butt cheeks, hands gripping the sides. He slaps my cheeks. It startles and arouses me.

I feel him. First his nose, then his face, then just his lips on my asshole. He reaches to finger my pussy. I hold one cheek open. He gets up, sticks his dick in me, and it feels so good I could cry. He's so poetic with his stroke game. I am experiencing so much pleasure, and I want Ursula to feel it, too.

I start to finger her again and watch her body move at me manipulating it. I stop when I start to cum again. I can't concentrate. I am trying to give his strokes back to him. I kiss Ursula, and we move off of her while he's inside of me. I yell in ecstasy.

It's time to dismount.

"Cum for me, Baby," I pant to Marcus.

He'll go all night if I don't stop him. I lay flat on my stomach on the bed. He cums hard when I lay like that. I feel the warmness of his sperm on my back. After more intense pounding, he cums again. I get up to suck dick just to see if I will be able to taste number three or at least get it in my face. I hit the jackpot and swallow the cum.

Ursula is in the corner smoking what is left of the of the blunt.

"Are you okay?" I ask her.

"Yeah, I'm good."

She lights a Kool. I crawl to her and get a cigarette.

I smile and say, "We're still friends, right?" I laugh and kiss her cheek.

"Yeah, Girl. Get from by me."

I crawl across the bed and to Marcus who is now half dressed in the hotel chair. I straddle him and kiss him. *I'm the only one still naked,* I think to myself. I get dressed.

I try to hold both their hands as we leave, and we take Ursula home.

Alise Merwin-Rasberry

In Search of a Midnight Snack

In search of a midnight snack.

It's late,

And the temptation to eat is there.

I've been following my diet:

Not eating too much,

Taking my vitamins,

Going to the gym.

There is ice cream in the fridge.

Then it hit me— something that would not
totally undo my good day.

252 milligrams of protein,

Vitamin C,

And B-12.

Only 5 to 25 calories.

I know you have to be up early,

But I'm hungry.

I put my butt in your lap to warn you I am coming.

Now I'm reaching and sliding under covers.

I like to feel it growing in my mouth.

You flinch,

And now I know you are awake.

Let me stick my face in your sack and get my fill.

I can tell you want to feed me.

You grab the back of my neck.

My tears come.

You cum.

Now we can go to bed satisfied.

THANK YOU FOR READING! PLEASE LEAVE A REVIEW WHEREVER REVIEWS ARE ACCEPTED.

Alise Merwin-Rasberry

Made in the USA
Coppell, TX
02 March 2026